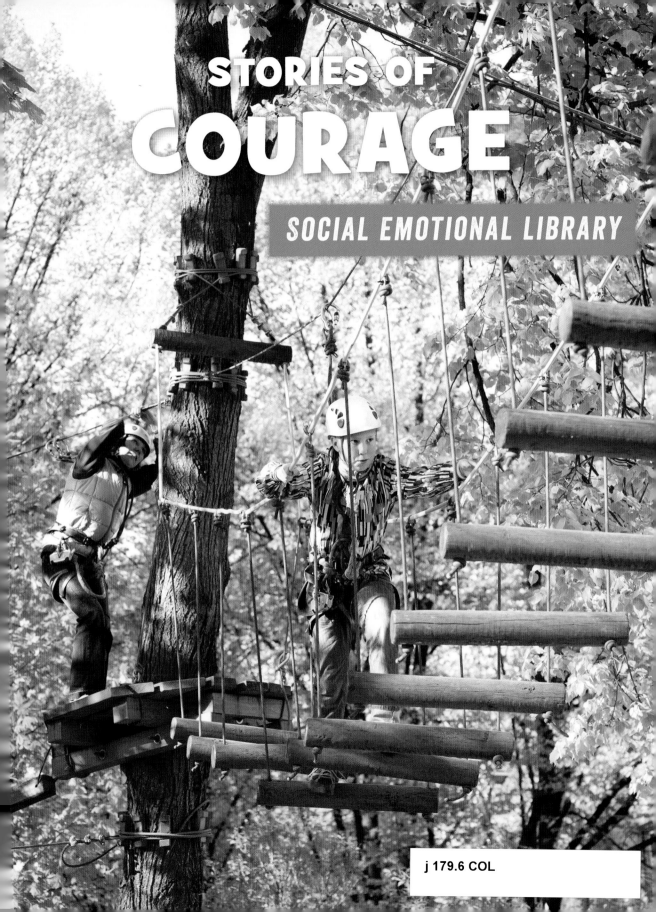

STORIES OF
COURAGE

SOCIAL EMOTIONAL LIBRARY

Published in the United States of America by Cherry Lake Publishing
Ann Arbor, Michigan
www.cherrylakepublishing.com

Content Adviser: Satta Sarmah Hightower, www.sattasarmah.com
Reading Adviser: Marla Conn MS, Ed., Literacy specialist, Read-Ability, Inc.

Photo Credits: ©Serge-Kazakov/iStock Images, cover, 1; ©mbolina/Shutterstock Images, 5; ©Wikimedia, 7; ©Jai Raj/
Wikimedia, 8; ©yakub88/Shutterstock Images, 11; ©Philip Willcocks/Shutterstock Images, 13; ©Alessia Pierdomenico/
Shutterstock Images, 15; ©tusharkoley/Shutterstock Images, 16; ©Gil.K/Shutterstock Images, 17; ©Toscanini/Shutterstock
Images, 18; ©Joseph Sohm/Shutterstock Images, 21; ©Wikimedia, 22; ©anyaivanova/Shutterstock Images, 25; ©Jeremy
Gilbert/Wikimedia, 26; ©dikobraziy/Shutterstock Images, 27; ©Pavel1964/Shutterstock Images, 28

Library of Congress Cataloging-in-Publication Data
Names: Colby, Jennifer, 1971- author.
Title: Stories of courage / by Jennifer Colby.
Description: Ann Arbor : Cherry Lake Publishing, [2018] | Series: Social emotional library |
    Audience: Grade 4 to 6. | Includes bibliographical references and index.
Identifiers: LCCN 2017035923 | ISBN 9781534107458 (hardcover) | ISBN 9781534109438 (pdf) |
    ISBN 9781534108448 (pbk.) | ISBN 9781534120426 (hosted ebook)
Subjects: LCSH: Courage—Biography—Juvenile literature.
Classification: LCC BJ1533.C8 C64 2018 | DDC 179/.6—dc23
LC record available at https://lccn.loc.gov/2017035923

Cherry Lake Publishing would like to acknowledge the work of The Partnership for 21st Century Learning.
Please visit www.p21.org for more information.

Printed in the United States of America
Corporate Graphics

ABOUT THE AUTHOR

Jennifer Colby is a school librarian in Michigan. She doesn't consider herself very
courageous, but is inspired by the stories of others to stand up for what is right and just.

TABLE OF CONTENTS

CHAPTER 1

What Is Courage?

Has anybody ever called you brave? What does it mean to be courageous? To be brave or courageous can mean many things. To have courage means that you can triumph over something that is difficult or challenging for you. Speaking in front of a group of people takes courage. You are also brave if you stand up for something you think is right. Helping a friend with a problem at school shows bravery. There are many stories of courage—all showing different types of bravery.

Showing courage can be difficult.

CHAPTER 2

Sergeant Stubby

Have you ever met a brave dog? Sometimes dogs will save a household from being robbed or wake up a family if they smell the smoke of a house fire. But have you ever heard of a dog that went to war? A dog adopted by an Army **infantry** unit during World War I became one of the most famous dogs of all time, known for his courage under fire.

In 1917, an infantry unit training for war on Yale University's campus adopted a terrier found wandering around. Stubby, so named for his short tail, was trained by the soldiers to identify military sound signals and participate in drills. He even developed his own paw "salute." When the unit was was sent overseas, Private Robert Conroy stowed Stubby away. But the commanding

Stubby's jacket carried medals he earned for his bravery.

officer in the unit discovered the dog. After Stubby gave the commander a salute, he was allowed to stay with the unit.

Stubby served with the infantry unit for the next 18 months in the trenches of France. Not only did the dog boost **morale**, he also saved the lives of the men in his unit. After being injured by a gas attack, he had become extremely sensitive to the smell of it. When he sniffed the faint scent of an approaching gas attack, he would run in the trenches barking at and biting soldiers to wake them up and put on their gas masks. A specialized gas mask was made for Stubby to protect him from further attacks.

In memory of Stubby, a brick was placed at the Liberty Memorial in Kansas City.

Trained to recognize English when spoken, Stubby would identify injured and lost soldiers. Then, he would bark until other soldiers could come and help. He had more sensitive hearing than humans, and he would whine when he heard the whistle of an incoming **artillery** shell. He was also responsible for catching a German spy. When the spy approached Stubby, the dog heard the man's language and put his ears back and barked. When the spy ran, Stubby chased after him and bit at his heels, knocking the spy down. Stubby continued attacking the spy until American soldiers arrived.

Stubby was injured again by **shrapnel** from a small bomb. After surgery, he was taken to a hospital to recover. While there, he boosted the morale of injured soldiers. By the end of the war, he had been in 17 battles and had earned the rank of sergeant—the first dog to do so. He even had a specially tailored uniform jacket.

After the war, Stubby led a parade of American troops as they passed President Woodrow Wilson. Later in his life, he met two more presidents in the White House: Warren G. Harding and Calvin Coolidge. Stubby was recognized for his courage on the battlefield and received many medals for heroism, including one from the Humane Society. He was also given memberships to the YMCA and the American Legion. When Robert Conroy began studying law at Georgetown University, Stubby became the university's sports mascot—and he was the inspiration for the school's Hoya Bulldog today. Stubby's uniform jacket is part of a World War I exhibit at the Smithsonian National Museum of American History. In 1926, Sergeant Stubby died of old age.

CHAPTER 3

Sir Nicholas Winton

Courage takes many forms. Sometimes it can mean putting your life in danger, but sometimes it can be solving a problem when no one else takes action. Sir Nicholas Winton is remembered for the noble actions he took before the start of World War II. He showed courage by helping **Jewish** people in Czechoslovakia when no one else would help.

Nicholas Wertheim was born in London on May 19, 1909. His parents were former German Jews. They had converted to Christianity and changed their name to Winton in order to blend in with the English community. In December 1938, Nicholas Winton, now a young businessman, was planning a ski vacation when a friend who worked for a **refugee** organization asked him to come to Prague, Czechoslovakia. His friend thought Winton might find the situation "interesting."

Frank Meisler and Arie Oviada sculpted bronze statues of the children Winton saved.

That spring, following Nazi Party leader Adolf Hitler's orders, Germany had taken over Austria. Hitler also wanted to control a nearby area called the Sudetenland. The other countries wanted to avoid war. Therefore, in the fall of 1938, Germany, Italy, France, and Britain agreed to give the Sudetenland to Germany. Soon Hitler's army **persecuted** Jews who lived there. They sent Jews to **concentration camps**. Jewish families wanted to leave but knew that getting out together was impossible. Only their children had a chance to escape.

Winton spent his two-week "holiday" hatching a plan with one aim: to get as many Jewish children out of Czechoslovakia as fast as possible. He had no experience with assisting refugees, but he had a strong desire to help. The first 20 Jewish children left Prague by train on March 14, 1939. The next day, German troops occupied Prague and the rest of Czechoslovakia, which made travel very difficult. The Nazi police distrusted and followed Winton. At great risk to himself, he bribed, or gave money, to the Nazis so they wouldn't stop his plan. He could have been arrested.

Still, over the spring and summer of 1939, seven trains with over 600 children traveled through Europe to the Netherlands. There, they took a ferry to awaiting adoptive families in England. A ninth train was scheduled to leave on September 1, 1939, but that was the day World War II began. Germany invaded Poland, and the children never left. At the time, no other group planned to rescue Jews in the area.

After the war, Winton never spoke much about his actions to save Jewish children. Then in 1988, he was on a British television program and was surprised to learn that the dozens of adults on the program with him were actually the children he had rescued.

His story was shared around the world, and he was honored for his actions. Winton was knighted by Queen Elizabeth II in

Winton was awarded the Order of the White Lion, the Czech Republic's highest honor.

2003 and was awarded the highest honor of the Czech Republic, the Order of the White Lion, in 2014.

Winton died in 2015 at the age of 106. Almost 78,000 Czech Jews were killed during the **Holocaust**, but his **moral** courage saved the lives of 669 Jewish children. Winton's son credited his father for influencing him and said, "It is about encouraging people to make a difference and not waiting for something to be done or waiting for someone else to do it." In 2014, it was estimated that **descendants** of the original 669 children numbered around 15,000.

CHAPTER 4

Nelson Mandela

Some people are very brave for one moment in time, but others are courageous for many years. Showing bravery throughout a long struggle is a sign of courage. Nelson Mandela was in prison for almost 30 years for his beliefs and actions, and was a courageous inspiration to the world.

Born in South Africa in 1918, Rolihlahla Mandela was given the first name "Nelson" while attending a Methodist school. As a student, Mandela was more interested in learning about native African culture and history than the English history he was being taught. South Africa was part of the British Empire and was **segregated**, so Mandela attended an all-black college. He soon became involved in a **boycott** against the quality of

Rolihlahla means "pulling the branch of a tree," or, "troublemaker."

food served at the school and was suspended. He never returned.

In 1941, he began working as a clerk for a lawyer sympathetic to the African National Congress (ANC), a group that supported equal rights for black people in South Africa. Studying to become a lawyer himself, Mandela became more involved with **social justice** causes, including boycotts, protests, and **strikes** against white-**minority** rule. In 1950, a new party of government came to power in South Africa. It established a system of **apartheid**, which permitted racial inequality through **discrimination**

The word "apartheid" is an Afrikaans word which originates from the Dutch language.

and segregation. In 1952, Mandela was arrested for speaking to a group that was protesting the government. After his release, he opened a law firm and defended many black clients who were mistreated and harmed by the police under the government's apartheid laws.

For many years, Mandela, with the help of the ANC, fought against apartheid. In 1964, he was convicted of government **sabotage** and was in prison for a total of 27 years. During that time, he endured periods of hard labor and physical and mental

Johannesburg is South Africa's largest city.

Mandela stayed in Robben Island Maximum Security Prison for 18 years.

abuse. Public knowledge of his long prison sentence made him the face of the anti-apartheid movement, though the black people of South Africa continued to suffer under apartheid.

Changes in South African and world politics led to Mandela's release in 1990. Through peaceful discussions, he and the white minority government ended apartheid. Because of the success of these talks, he was awarded the Nobel Peace Prize in 1993. In 1994, the country's first democratic election selected Mandela as South Africa's president, signaling the end of apartheid. Mandela's main goal as president was national **reconciliation**—to unify whites and blacks. He developed many social and economic programs to reduce inequality between both races.

Mandela once said, "I learned that courage was not the absence of fear, but the triumph over it. The brave man is not he who does not feel afraid, but he who conquers that fear." Nelson Mandela suffered for many years for his belief that all men and women should be treated equally regardless of their race. It was his triumph over his fear that enabled him to continue on to succeed in his fight for the equal rights of black South Africans.

Are You Courageous?

Have you ever stood up for what is right? If you have, then you are courageous. Maybe you stood up for a friend who was being bullied on the playground. Or maybe you helped a small animal that was suffering. Remember, though, it is important to consider the safety of a situation before you act. The safety of yourself and others should be your first concern.

CHAPTER 5

Rosa Parks

It only takes a moment of bravery to cause a series of events that can change the way people live. Rosa Parks's moment of resistance on a bus ride home began a movement that helped to **integrate** the South. Her uncommon courage inspired others to stand up for themselves as well.

On December 1, 1955, Parks was on a Montgomery, Alabama, bus and refused to give up her seat to a white man who had just boarded. Like the rest of the South, Montgomery was segregated. Local laws forced the separation of whites and blacks in all facilities—schools, restaurants, movie theaters, courthouses, libraries—as well as on buses. For many years, African-Americans were expected to follow these laws. A black person who used the

The bus that Rosa Parks rode still exists today.

"whites only" facilities or spoke out against segregation would be arrested.

Rosa Parks had just finished a long day working as a seamstress on that December evening. She was already sitting in the "**colored**" section of the bus when the "white" section filled up and another white person entered the bus. Though Parks understood the bus driver could have her arrested, she refused to give up her seat. She knew the bus driver well. He once forced her to exit the bus after she had entered from the front, demanded that she enter from the rear, and then sped off before she could

After her first arrest, Parks was arrested a second time
for her role in the bus boycott.

board the bus again. Parks also knew that the driver carried a
gun. "The time had just come when I had been pushed as far as
I could stand to be pushed, I suppose. I had decided that I would
have to know, once and for all, what rights I had as a human
being, and a citizen," she said later about the incident.

Parks was arrested and soon became the face of the anti-
segregation movement in Montgomery. Her arrest started
protests and a bus boycott in the city, which lasted over a year.
Black passengers refused to ride the city buses until they were
desegregated. To sustain the boycott, black leaders organized

carpools, and black taxi cab drivers reduced their fares for black riders. Many black residents chose to walk instead. Finally, the US Supreme Court ordered the city of Montgomery to integrate its bus system.

Rosa Parks's simple act of courage earned her honor and recognition as a civil rights activist. Though she avoided the spotlight, she worked behind the scenes for the rest of her life to support civil rights leaders and to raise awareness for social justice causes. In 1996, she was awarded the Presidential Medal of Freedom. And in 1999, she was awarded the Congressional Gold Medal for being the "mother of the civil rights movement."

Courage in the Workplace

Being courageous is necessary for having a good career. For example, bravery lets people overcome fears like speaking out about something, whether it's an opinion or if someone is bothering you. Have you ever had a really good idea but you were too shy to share it? Chances are your boss would love to hear new ideas. What do you do if a coworker ever makes you feel sad or uncomfortable? By being courageous, you can let this person, a trusted co-worker, or your boss know how you feel and resolve the situation so you can be happy at work.

CHAPTER 6

Terry Fox

Born on July 28, 1958, in Winnipeg, Manitoba, Canada, Terry Fox was an enthusiastic athlete. He played rugby, soccer, and basketball as a child. In college, Fox beat out more accomplished basketball players, and his determination earned him a spot on the junior varsity basketball team. But in the winter of 1976, he felt a pain in his right knee. He ignored it until basketball season was over, and three months later was diagnosed with osteosarcoma, an aggressive type of bone cancer. His leg had to be amputated, he endured 16 months of chemotherapy treatment, and he was told that he had a 50 percent chance of survival. Fox understood the importance of cancer research and was inspired to raise money for the Canadian Cancer Society.

After his surgery and treatment, Fox was determined to run

Some fundraising supports cancer research.

across Canada to bring awareness to cancer research. He trained for over a year aiming to run a marathon per day to complete his goal. His heart was set on fundraising for research, and he once said, "Somewhere the hurting must stop … and I was determined to take myself to the limit for this cause." His Marathon of Hope began on April 12, 1980, in St. John's, Newfoundland, Canada. He filled a container with water from the Atlantic Ocean and planned to pour it in the Pacific Ocean when he arrived there months later. Fox's goal was to raise $23 million—one dollar for every Canadian citizen.

On average, Fox ran 26 miles (42 km) each day during the Marathon of Hope.

Fox stopped running outside of Thunder Bay, Ontario.

Because of his **prosthetic** leg, Fox ran with an interesting hop-step gait. He also suffered blisters and bone bruises, but found that after 20 minutes of running, he could continue on through the pain. At first, Fox was disappointed with the attention his campaign received. Few crowds showed up to cheer him on, and only a few thousand dollars came in. But after a few weeks, the Canadian news started following his trek. He met Canada's prime minister, famous athletes, and thousands of people along the way. By July 11, he had reached Toronto, Ontario, and had raised more than $100,000.

Today, many marathons help fund medical research.

Terry's courageous journey came to an end on September 1. After almost 5 months and 3,339 miles (5,373.6 kilometers) of running daily, he was short of breath and had chest pain. He was taken to the hospital and learned that his cancer had returned and spread to his lungs. He had already raised $1.7 million, but with news of the run ending, a nationwide telethon was held and raised an additional $10.5 million. Donations continued coming in, and by the next spring Fox's campaign had received $23 million. After months of cancer treatment, Fox died on June 28, 1981.

In September 1980, Terry Fox became a Companion of the Order of Canada for displaying the "highest degree of merit to Canada and humanity." Running days on end through rain, gale-force winds, and tremendous pain, Terry Fox's commitment to his cause required true courage despite the hardship he experienced along the way.

What Have You Learned About Courage?

There are many types of bravery. Courage can be demonstrated despite great pain, suffering, and hardship. Some people's courage is recognized by all, but some people's courage is never known. Courageous people do what they believe is right. It is important to consider the consequences of courageous acts—the safety of all should be a first priority. Being brave can inspire other people to stand up for themselves and others.

Think About It

How Can You Become More Courageous?

Sometimes it is hard to be brave. Many times, being brave means speaking out when others do not. We all have a hard time calling attention to ourselves, but sometimes it is necessary. Showing courage, however, doesn't always mean being noticed. You can be brave just by supporting what you believe in. Find a cause that you believe in and ask how you can help. You can show courage by supporting a worthy goal.

For More Information

Further Reading

Barber, Terry. *Terry Fox.* Edmonton, AB: Grass Roots Press, 2012.

Helfand, Lewis. *Nelson Mandela: The Unconquerable Soul.* New Delhi: Campfire, 2011.

Rogak, Lisa. *The Dogs of War: The Courage, Love, and Loyalty of Military Working Dogs.* New York: St. Martin's Griffin, 2011.

Websites

History—Nelson Mandela
https://www.history.com/topics/nelson-mandela
Check out this biographical website about Nelson Mandela.

The Henry Ford—What If I Don't Move to the Back of the Bus?
https://www.thehenryford.org/explore/stories-of-innovation/what-if/rosa-parks/
This website highlights the Rosa Parks story and the famous bus behind it.

United States Holocaust Memorial Museum—The Holocaust: A Learning Site for Students
https://www.ushmm.org/learn/students/the-holocaust-a-learning-site-for-students
This website presents an overview of the Holocaust through photographs, maps, and videos.

GLOSSARY

apartheid (uh-PAHR-tyde) a former social system in South Africa in which black people, Indian South Africans, and people of mixed descent did not have the same political and economic rights as white people and were forced to live separately from whites

artillery (ahr-TIL-uh-ree) large guns that are used to shoot over a great distance

boycott (BOY-kot) organized act of refusing to buy or use something

colored (KUHL-erd) an old-fashioned and offensive term for anything related to race other than white

concentration camps (kahn-suhn-TRAY-shuhn KAMPS) types of prisons where large numbers of people are kept during a war and forced to live in very bad conditions

descendants (dih-SEN-duhnts) people who are related to a person or group of people who lived in the past

discrimination (dis-krim-ih-NAY-shuhn) the practice of unfairly treating a group of people

Holocaust (HAH-luh-kawst) the killing of millions of European Jews and others by the Nazis during World War II

infantry (IN-fuhn-tree) the foot soldiers of an army

integrate (IN-tuh-grayt) to end a policy that keeps people of different races apart

Jewish (JOO-ish) relating to Judaism, a religion that believes in God

minority (muh-NOR-ih-tee) a smaller group of people of a particular race, ethnic group, or religion living among a larger group of people

moral (MOR-uhl) relating to what is right and wrong in human behavior

morale (muh-RAL) a group's feelings of enthusiasm

persecuted (PUR-suh-kyoot-ed) treated cruelly or unfairly especially because of race, religious, or political beliefs

prosthetic (pros-THET-ik) an artificial device that replaces a missing or injured part of the body

reconciliation (rek-uhn-sil-ee-AY-shuhn) the act of causing two groups to become friendly again after a disagreement or fight

refugee (REF-yoo-jee) someone who has been forced to leave a country because of war or for religious or political reasons

sabotage (SAB-uh-taj) to purposefully cause the failure of something

segregated (SEG-rih-gay-tid) separated by race

shrapnel (SHRAP-nuhl) small metal pieces that scatter outwards from an exploding bomb, shell, or mine

social justice (SOH-shuhl JUHS-tis) based on concepts of human rights and equality, it concerns opportunities, privileges, and wealth in a society

strikes (STRIKES) periods of time when workers stop work in order to force an employer or government to agree to their demands

INDEX